D1265284

The GRITTY Little Lamb

written by **Dan Allbaugh**   illustrated by **Anil Yap**

Publisher's Cataloguing-in-Publication Data
Names: Allbaugh, Dan, author. | Yap, Anil, illustrator.
Title: The gritty little lamb / by Dan Allbaugh ; illustrated by Anil Yap.
Description: First edition. | Urbandale, IA : Green Meeple Books, [2020] | Audience: Ages 0-6.
Summary: In this book with rhyming text, a lamb's parents educate him about the value of practice, perseverance, and attitude to achieve his goal which, for right now, is beating dad at a game.
Identifiers: LCCN 2020917683 | ISBN: 978-1-7357708-4-0 (paperback) | 978-1-7357708-1-9 (hardback) | 978-1-7357708-0-2 (ebook)
Subjects: LCSH: Games—Juvenile fiction. | Sheep—Juvenile fiction. | Determination (Personality trait)—Juvenile fiction. | Stories in rhyme. | Picture books. | CYAC: Stories in rhyme. | Games—Fiction. | Sheep—Fiction. | LCGFT: Stories in rhyme. | Picture books.
Classification: LCC PZ8.3.A4533844 Gri 2020 | DDC [E] — dc23

Book design by Michele N. Tupper | Michele Design Works
Typeset in Century Gothic
The illustrations in the book were rendered in Autodesk Sketchbook.

PRINTED IN THE UNITED STATES OF AMERICA
10 9 8 7 6 5 4 3 2 1

Green Meeple Books
3206 146th St, Urbandale, Iowa, 50323

greenmeeplebooks.com

For Elliott and Andrew,
May all your days be filled with as much joy as you give me;
May your wonder continue to outpace your satisfaction;
May you always choose kindness, remain humble and stay determined.
You are infinitely capable of all that you dream of and hope for.
I love you bigger than the whole universe.
– D.A.

To Him,
To all the dreams, hopes and aspired endeavors,
may this be a start of something new—something fruitful.
— A.Y

Little Lambie loved to play.
If he had his way, he'd play all day.

Building towers. Playground slides.
Jumping. Hanging. Wagon rides.

Blowing bubbles. Climbing trees.
Nearly all activities.
When asked his favorite he exclaims,

"There's nothing
I love more
than games!"

"Come and join me at the table.
All are welcome. Tell the stable!
I've got plenty of room to spare.
Don't stand and stare.

Pull up a chair!"

From the start, the very beginning,
his heart was filled by the joy of winning.

There's not an animal he couldn't beat.
(But he loved to win,
          so they let him cheat.)

Then one day he played with Dad
who played it straight, which made Lamb mad.

"I've played this since
my days in school.

You're not playing
by the rules."

Daddy understood his pain.
He paused a moment -
then explained,

"Son, I've played this game for years.
I've lost my share. And shed some tears.

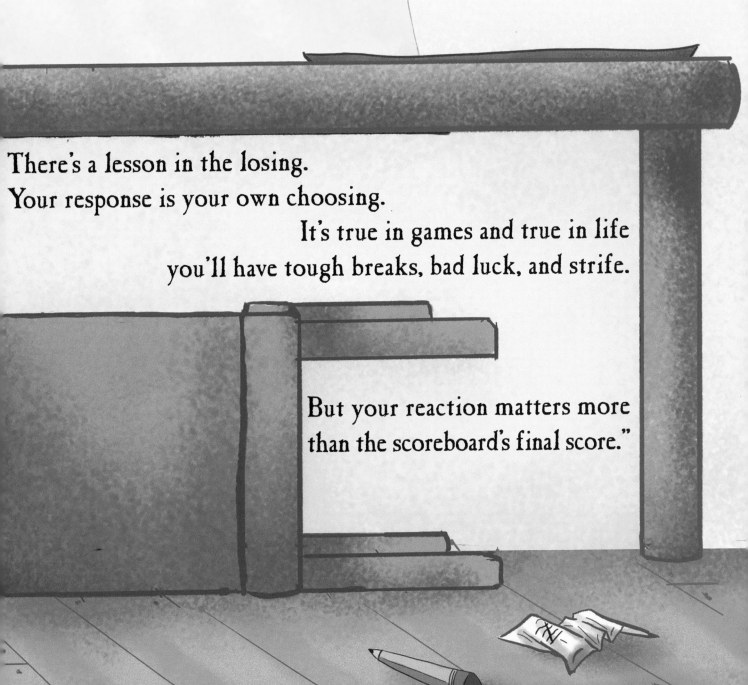

There's a lesson in the losing.
Your response is your own choosing.

It's true in games and true in life
you'll have tough breaks, bad luck, and strife.

But your reaction matters more
than the scoreboard's final score."

Lambie knew that dads are shrewd,
so rearranged his attitude.
Now Little Lamb was filled with drive.
Confident that he would thrive.

"I'll study hard and learn the rules.
I'll excel. I have the tools!
Next time we play, I'll go farther.
I'll beat you. I'll work harder."

Very quickly he improved.
Mommy helped to show him moves.

"Stick with it," she told Lambie.
"Practice. Practice. That's the key."

But all the hours started mounting.
Way too many (and sheep love counting).

"It's so much work,"
Lambie said,

"I can't do it."
Then hung his head.

Mom's next words kept him going -
helped him see that he was growing.

"Remember kid, you weren't born talking.
At twelve months you started walking.
When you fell, you weren't done.

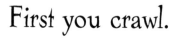

First you crawl.

Then walk.

Then run.

It all happens bit by bit.

But you never get there if you quit.
So when you say,

'I can't do it.'

Don't forget

. to add a

'yet'."

Lambie knew that moms are wise.
He'd listen well to score the prize.

"I can't give up
and quit on me.
I'd never know
how great I'd be!"

So every day he trains some more
striving for a higher score.
A rematch will be his finest hour.
All this practice gives him power.

The day arrived when he felt ready.

"I can win!

Prepare confetti!"

He challenged Dad
to that same game -

His passion burning like a flame.

His hard work showed for all to see.
The game was as close
as close could be.

"The final move comes down to me
I will secure the victory!"

Lambie squeaked by with the win.
His dad gave him a sheepish grin.

"Son," he said
            "I'm proud of you.

You thought to quit
            but saw it through.

I have had my share of wins
but that's not where the joy begins.
On that journey of improvement,

it's fun to find
that you CAN do it.

Grow the biggest watermelon?
Tell the funniest joke worth tellin'?

Ride a skateboard?

Surf a wave?

You can do them if you crave.

Have bigger dreams?

Make them yours.

You could dig up dinosaurs!

Or take a trip
through space to Mars.
Then you'd live among the stars.

With any passion you pursue
your success is up to you.

Whatever you may want to be,
don't quit, and you'll achieve your dreams.

You can do it...

Just not yet.

You WILL do it.

I'll take that bet."

SAVE THE SHEEP

A hungry wolf is starting to creep!

Build a fence. Save the sheep!

RULES

1. Each turn, draw a line or use an object to connect two horizontally or vertically adjacent dots to make a fence line.

2. Making the fourth line of a box fences in a sheep, earning you a point. When you fence in a sheep you must move again.

3. Lines are drawn until all sheep are safe and fenced in. The player with the most fenced in sheep wins!

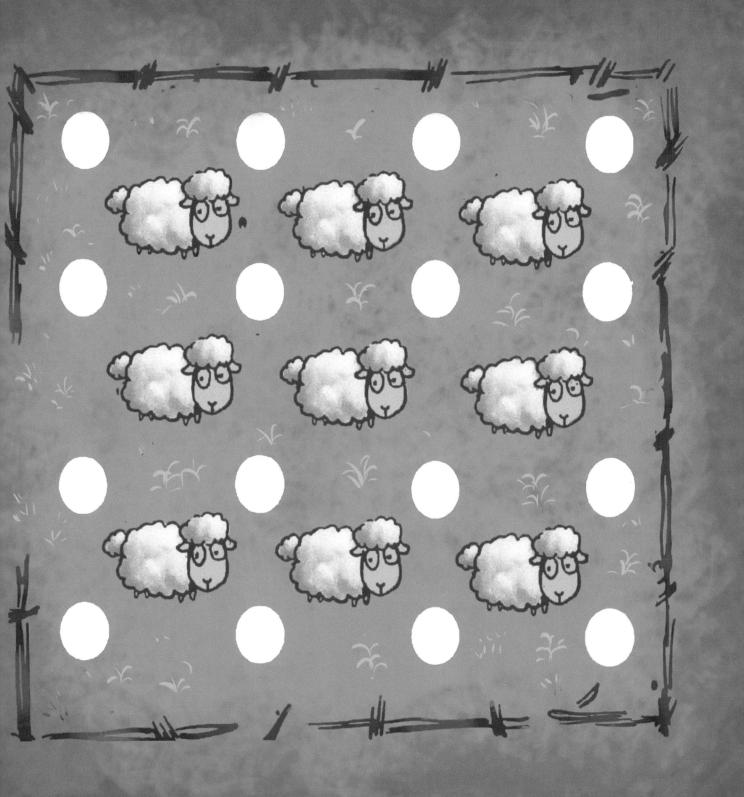

CPSIA information can be obtained
at www.ICGtesting.com
Printed in the USA
BVHW021721230321
603277BV00010B/139